Published by Ladybird Books Ltd.
A Penguin Company
Penguin Books Ltd, 80 Strand, London, WC2R 0RL, England
Penguin Books Australia Ltd, Camberwell, Victoria, Australia
Penguin Books (NZ), cnr Airborne and Rosedale Roads, Albany, Auckland 1310, New Zealand

Manufactured in Italy

www.ladybird.co.uk

It was harvest time on Ant Island, and for the first time, Princess Atta was in charge. Her mother, the queen, was getting old, and Atta was training to take her place.

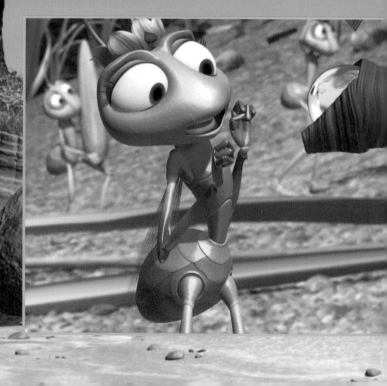

Suddenly a young ant named Flik rushed over, bringing his latest invention with him.

But Atta wasn't impressed. Flik's inventions were always trouble and they never worked.

"Just pick grain like everyone else, Flik," she sighed.

An alarm sounded. Hopper and his gang of grasshoppers were coming! Quickly, the ants scattered.

Every year, the ants had to leave a share of their harvest on an offering stone for the greedy grasshoppers. This year the offering stone was full – but in his rush to get away, Flik bumped into the stone and knocked it over. All the grain fell over the side of the cliff!

Hopper was furious. "I want double the amount now," he snarled at the trembling ants. "If you don't collect it for us before the last leaf falls, none of you will be safe!" With that he led his gang away.

The whole colony was scared, but Flik had another idea. He would go to the city to find bigger bugs to fight Hopper.

Atta agreed to let Flik go – but only to stop him causing more trouble with his mad ideas.

Dot liked Flik. He was always kind to her, and cheered her up when she felt sad about being so small. Dot and two boy ants went to see Flik off.

"My dad says he's going to die," one of the boys sneered.

"He's not going to die," Dot declared. "He's going to get the bestest, toughest bugs ever!" She waved to Flik as he sailed away on a dandelion seed.

In the city, a group of performing bugs sat in a bar made from an old paint tin. They were feeling sad. P. T. Flea had just fired them from his circus.

Some flies started teasing Francis the ladybird and his friends. To scare them off, Francis grabbed Slim the stick insect

and waved him around like a sword. "Stand back!" he shouted. "We're the greatest warriors in the land!"

Flik walked in just in time to hear the word 'warriors' and ran up to watch the fight. But things were getting out of hand. The circus bugs turned and ran, tipping the bar over. They landed on the flies. Flik thought they'd won.

"I've been looking for bugs with your talent!" he said.

Thinking Flik wanted to book their act, the circus bugs happily accepted his invitation to Ant Island.

"Flik! I knew you could do it!" shouted Dot, when Flik returned with the circus bugs.

The other ants were afraid of the big bugs so Francis said, "When your grasshopper friends get here, we're going to knock 'em dead!" The ants were overjoyed.

The ant colony held a feast to welcome the circus bugs. Some of the ant children put on a play about the battle with Hopper.

Rosie the spider was worried. "Is that us fighting?" she whispered. "We're only circus performers!"

Suddenly Flik understood what Rosie was saying. He hurried the circus bugs outside. Dot saw Flik leave and followed him. But she couldn't hear what he was saying. She grabbed a dandelion seed and floated nearer.

The circus bugs thought Flik had tricked them, and they wanted to leave. Flik was trying to make them stay when a bird appeared.

"Run!" screamed Flik.

But little Dot was right in the bird's path! The princess let go of the dandelion and fell towards the ground. Quickly, Francis flew over and caught her. They landed in a crack in the riverbed. Poor Francis was knocked unconscious, and his leg was trapped under a stone.

While Heimlich the caterpillar and Slim distracted the bird, Flik and the others rescued Francis and Dot. Rosie carried them to safety in a web.

The whole ant colony cheered. The circus bugs were heroes!

The amazing rescue gave Flik an idea. Even Hopper was terrified of birds. They could build a mechanical bird to fool him and frighten the grasshoppers away!

Work began at once. The ants and circus bugs worked together, and everyone was filled with excitement. Flik's newest invention would scare off Hopper and his gang once and for all!

At last the bird was ready. There were cheers as the creature was raised up into a tree. The ants were ready for Hopper now!

Meanwhile, in their hide-out, Hopper and his lazy brother Molt were arguing.

"We're having a good time here," said Molt. "Why should we go back to Ant Island?"

"Those ants outnumber us," growled Hopper. "If we don't show them who's boss, they'll take over! Now, let's ride!"

That evening P. T. Flea arrived at the ant colony, looking for the circus bugs. He wanted them back for his new show.

When P. T. Flea told the colony that the brave 'warriors' were just performers, Atta and the queen told the circus bugs to go.

"I want you to leave, too," Atta told Flik. "And this time, don't ever come back!"

Dot tried to follow him, but the queen stopped her. As Flik and his friends left, the last leaf fell.

Just a few hours later, the grasshoppers arrived. When Hopper found the offering stone empty, he looked for the ants' own food store.

"No! We'll starve!" Atta protested.

Shoving her into the food pile, Hopper grabbed the queen. "No ant sleeps until we get every scrap of food on the island," he snarled.

Dot and the Blueberry scout troop
were hiding, and they overheard the
grasshopper gang talking.

"We'll work 'em till they drop,"
laughed one of them. "Then we'll
squish the queen!"

Dot raced off to find Flik and the circus bugs.

"You've got to help us!" she gasped. "Hopper's going to squish my mum!"

The circus bugs still thought Flik's bird idea would work, but Flik was too miserable to try.

Then Dot reminded Flik how he had encouraged her when she'd felt small and helpless. Flik looked up and smiled at his friend.

"All right!" he cried. "We'll do it!" And they began to make a plan.

That evening, as the grasshoppers feasted on the ants' grain, a bug circus parade rumbled into sight.

"What's going on?" Hopper demanded.

"We are here to entertain you!" Manny announced.

The grasshoppers were busy watching Manny's act and didn't see Flik climbing into the bird machine.

All at once the bird flapped out of the tree. From inside the creature, Flik and the Blueberries made loud screeching noises. The rest of the ants ran around, pretending to be scared.

Screaming in terror, the grasshoppers ran for cover. Everything was going as planned, until P. T. Flea set fire to the bird. He was trying to 'save' his circus bugs.

When Flik and the Blueberries crawled from the blazing bird, Hopper knew he'd been tricked.

But Flik bravely stood up to Hopper, and the ants and circus bugs joined him. The gang backed off, and Hopper stood alone.

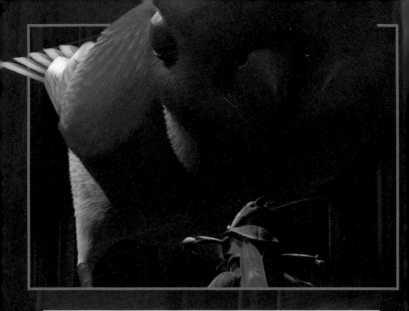

Suddenly huge raindrops splashed down. As everyone ran for cover, Hopper grabbed Flik. But Atta snatched him away. Hopper chased after them, following Flik to the sparrow's nest. He thought Flik had built another bird, and before he realised that the sparrow was real, it was too late. Hopper looked up just in time to see the bird heading straight for him.

When spring arrived, the circus
bugs prepared to leave Ant Island.
Princess Atta was now in charge, and
Flik had a new job as the colony's
inventor. Thanks to Flik's courage,
Hopper would never bother the
colony again.